D0410604

STAR WARS™

MEET THE VILLAINS

STORMTROOPERS

BRENT LIBRARIES	
EAL	
91120000402231	
Askews & Holts	03-May-2019
J791.437 JUNIOR NON-	£4.99

STAR WARS™

MEET THE VILLAINS

STORMTROOPERS

Written by
Emma Grange

Are all stormtroopers men?

How many stormtroopers work on the Death Star?

Where do stormtroopers go on holiday?

Which are the tallest troopers?

What is inside their helmets?

Find out the answers to these questions and many more inside!

Who are these soldiers?

Stormtroopers. These are special soldiers working for the **rulers of the galaxy.** Spot them on many planets. They wear **white armour** and look **fierce!**

Why are they needed?

To seize control of as many planets as possible! The stormtroopers are first commanded by **Emperor Palpatine.**

He creates an evil Empire to rule the galaxy. When a new threat, the **First Order,** rises up, they use a vast army of stormtroopers, too!

Emperor Palpatine

Who fights the stormtroopers?

The rebels do. They want the galaxy to be free of the Empire. The stormtroopers **work for the Empire,** so the rebels plan to **fight** the stormtroopers.

8

Are stormtroopers good in a fight?

Yes and no. Stormtroopers are **highly trained,** but they can be beaten. If their foes, such as warrior Chirrut, are **quick,** they can **trip troopers up** or **surprise** them from behind!

How many types of stormtroopers are there?

Many! The stormtoopers have different names and armour for all their many missions. **Snow, sand, mud or sea,** stormtroopers are prepared for everything!

Snowtrooper

Sandtrooper

Mudtrooper

Shoretrooper

Which troopers work in mud?

Mudtroopers. These soldiers are also known as **swamp troopers.** They often work on **dirty** planets with **poisonous air,** so they wear **masks** to help them breathe.

Do stormtroopers like working in sand?

Not really! Troopers find it difficult to walk in the sand and it can get **very hot** inside their armour. Stormtroopers who work in **sandy, desert conditions** are called **sandtroopers.**

Why is this stormtrooper wearing a strange helmet?

This is a snowtrooper on an icy planet. The helmet has inbuilt **goggles** for looking at bright, light, snowy landscapes. The armour contains **heating controls** to keep the wearer **warm.**

What is a flametrooper?

A stormtrooper who can blast fire! These First Order soldiers carry weapons that can shoot **flames!** Their helmets protect them from the **heat** of the **fire.** Flametroopers are often found at the front of the action.

Who is this?

A scout trooper. Some stormtroopers have special jobs and special names. Scout troopers **investigate,** or **scout out,** enemy worlds. Keep a lookout for danger, scout trooper!

What is this vehicle?

A speeder bike. Stormtroopers **can't fly,** but with these vehicles they can **hover** above the ground! Speeder bikes can zoom away very fast, so they are good for **spying** in enemy territory.

17

How tall are stormtroopers?

They are average human size. Stormtroopers must also be physically fit and healthy.

Which are the tallest troopers?

Death troopers. These **scary-looking** soldiers dress all in black, train in **top secret** sites and work for important officers of the Empire only. At nearly 2 metres (6 feet 5 inches) tall, they **tower** over all the other troopers.

What material is stormtrooper armour made of?

Plastoid. This is a **special material** designed to protect stormtroopers from attacks. Each suit is formed of **18** overlapping armour pieces. This allows stormtroopers to move around freely.

What do they wear under their armour?

A black bodysuit. This layer is made of **stretchy** material that fits each stormtrooper like a **glove.**

Why are stormtroopers called "bucket heads"?

Because their helmets are shaped like buckets! This **nickname** is given to stormtroopers by the **rebels.** The rebels do not like stormtroopers!

Stormtrooper
FN-2187

When can stormtroopers take off their helmets?

Only when given permission.

Stormtroopers must look **professional** at all times.
Their helmets also provide **protection.**

What is inside their helmets?

All sorts of equipment.

Stormtroopers are hooked up to **communications** devices so that they can talk to one another. They also have **breathing** devices to pump in clean air.

Padding

Speaker

Breathing device

Stormtrooper helmet

What weapons do stormtroopers use?

Blasters! Stormtroopers' blasters are capable of **stunning** their opponents. For close-range combat, they also use **batons** and shields.

Baton

Blaster

Do they need any other equipment?

Quadnoculars! Stormtroopers must go out **on patrol.** They need to be able to search for enemies far away. Quadnoculars help them to see **far** into the **distance.**

How do stormtroopers get around?

Marching! Lots and lots of marching. Stormtroopers must learn how to march **quickly** no matter the weather and in very **straight** lines. **Left, right,** left, right!

What vehicles do they drive?

It depends. On a battlefield where stormtroopers need **height,** they drive **AT-STs** (All Terrain Scout Transports). They can **blast** their enemies from the cockpit, high off the ground.

AT-ST

What about on crowded city streets.

Tanks! On the busy streets of Jedha, stormtroopers called **tank troopers** drive big heavy tanks. They **trample** over anything in their path!

Do stormtroopers work with animals?

They do! On sandy planet Tatooine, stormtroopers ride **lizard creatures** called **dewbacks.** Sand gets stuck in the troopers' vehicles, but dewbacks cope well with the difficult terrain.

Why do these people all look the same?

They are clones! The Empire's first stormtroopers were **identical soldiers** known as **clones.** They were **programmed** to follow all the Empire's orders.

Where did clone troopers come from?

The planet Kamino.

Tall Kaminoans worked here. They used their scientific brains to produce a whole **factory** of clones for the Galactic Republic. The clones were then used by the Empire.

Who trained the clone troopers?

Jango Fett! The clones are exact **copies** of him. This makes him the best person to know how the troopers will **act** and **behave.**

Where do stormtroopers come from?

The Empire recruits them. Posters across the galaxy ask for **volunteers** to join the ranks. Stormtroopers must start their training when they are **young.** Would **you** like to join them?

Do stormtroopers have families?

Probably. But stormtroopers often have to leave their families behind and **travel** to **other planets.** Working as a stormtrooper can take them **far away** from home!

Recruitment poster

33

Where do stormtroopers train?

At Imperial Academies. One of these training camps is on the planet **Lothal.** Here young trainees, or **cadets,** must successfully **pass a series of tests** before they can **graduate** as official stormtroopers.

How much training do they do?

Lots and lots and lots of training!

Becoming a stormtrooper is hard work. Cadets must complete **obstacle courses,** do physical **exercises** and learn **battle tactics.**

Which rules must stormtroopers follow?

All of them! Stormtroopers must **never retreat,** must always **train hard** at everything and above all should remain **loyal to the Empire.**

What happens if stormtroopers break the rules?

They get punished. Often they are given lots of **nasty** and **boring** jobs to do. Some might get sent to work on the Empire's **drains,** for example. **Yuck!**

Where do stormtroopers go on holiday?

Scarif. This planet looks like a tropical paradise, but it hides a secret Empire base. Troopers who work here are called **shoretroopers.** Some people think working here is as easy as a trip to the beach!

39

Who do stormtroopers work for?

The Empire, then the First Order!

Under the Emperor's rule, **Darth Vader** orders the stormtroopers to **track down** and defeat the rebels. When the First Order controls the galaxy, General Hux **takes charge** of a new army.

Emperor Palpatine

Darth
Vader

General
Hux

How many stormtroopers work on the Death Star?

25,984! The Death Star is a **giant weapon** belonging to the Empire. It can destroy whole planets. It is also a **battle station.** The thousands of stormtroopers on-board must **protect it.**

How many stormtroopers can fit on a Star Destroyer?

More than 9,700. Star Destroyers are **triangle-shaped** ships belonging to important members of the Empire. They carry smaller ships on-board to **shuttle** stormtroopers off to battle.

Star Destroyer

45

Who have these stormtroopers captured?

This is Princess Leia. She is a rebel leader. Stormtroopers take her prisoner when they think she has **stolen** something from the Empire!

Who disguises themselves as stormtroopers?

Rebels do! Luke Skywalker and Han Solo dress up as stormtroopers to **fool the Empire** and **free** rebel prisoner Princess Leia! It works!

Who likes the stormtroopers?

Nobody! These furry guys are called **Ewoks.** When the stormtroopers invade their homeworld, they **fight back** to **stop them!** The Ewoks do not like the stormtroopers.

How can small creatures beat stormtroopers?

By working together! Ewoks are **small,** but they should not be **ignored.** They work as a team and use **sticks** and **stones** to beat the group of invading stormtroopers. Very **creative!**

What are these stormtroopers?

They work for the First Order. Their armour has been **strengthened** so that it gives greater protection. It is also more **flexible** so that stormtroopers can run and fight easily.

What is the First Order?

The new threat to the galaxy.

The Empire and Emperor Palpatine were **defeated** by the rebels. But soon a **new force,** called the First Order, rose in its place. It uses fierce stormtrooper too. These troopers must fight the **Resistance,** a group of rebel heroes trying to stop the First Order.

First Order
stormtrooper

49

Do stormtroopers have friends?

Some do. A lot of stormtroopers are too busy fighting to make friends. But if stormtroopers do make friends, then they can **stick together** during battles and **help each other out!** Trooper FN-2187 has a friend, and they fight side by side.

Can a stormtrooper ever quit?

Not easily. Anybody trying to escape is usually captured and brought straight back to base. Once you become a stormtrooper, you can **never** leave!

Who is FN-2187?

An unhappy stormtrooper. But not for long! When he realises how evil the First Order is, he decides to **run away.** He makes new rebel friends who call him **"Finn"** instead of FN-2187.

How does Finn escape?

He steals a TIE fighter! This ship belongs
to the First Order. Finn wants to get away as fast as possible,
so he helps a Resistance pilot steal the ship and they fly away!

Do stormtroopers have names?

Not usually. When someone becomes
a stormtrooper they normally give up
their name. In its place, they are given
a unique number.

How do stormtroopers get to battles?

On ships called transports.

Vehicles such as this Atmospheric Assault Lander (AAL) can carry up to **20** stormtroopers. When the **ramp** is lowered, the troopers race into battle.

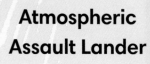

Atmospheric Assault Lander

What is a squad?

A group of 10 stormtroopers.

Stormtroopers **travel** and **fight** in their squads.

They look even more terrifying in vast numbers!

Are all stormtroopers men?

No! This is **Captain Phasma.** Her job is to train **young** stormtroopers, and she does not like her orders to be ignored. She is **determined** and **strong!**

How can you spot a leader?
Check their shoulders!

Stormtrooper leaders, or officers, often wear special shoulder pieces called **pauldrons.** This helps the troops spot who should be giving them orders. Different colours are used to show rank.

Officer's pauldron

What's next for the stormtroopers?

More fighting! The First Order sends hundreds of stormtroopers to the planet **Crait** to fight members of the **Resistance** group. Some of these new rebels manage to escape. The stormtroopers must now **try** to **find them!**

Glossary

Empire
A group of nations ruled over by one leader, who is called an Emperor.

First Order
An organisation that takes control of the galaxy when the Empire is defeated.

Force
A mysterious energy that can be used for good or for evil.

Galactic Republic
An elected government that rules many planets in the galaxy before it is replaced by the Empire.

Graduate
Successfully complete a course of study, often by passing exams or tests.

Imperial
Belonging to the Empire.

Loyal
Faithfully giving your support to a particular organisation or person.

Patrol
An expedition to keep watch over a certain area, often by guards or soldiers.

Rebel
Someone who rises up to fight against the current ruler.

Recruit
Encourage someone to sign up for something, such as the army.

Retreat
Run away from your enemy on the battlefield.

Stun
Knock someone unconscious.

Penguin
Random
House

Senior Editors Ruth Amos and Emma Grange
Senior Designers Lynne Moulding and Clive Savage
Project Art Editor Jon Hall
Designers David McDonald and Stefan Georgiou
Senior Pre-Production Producer Jennifer Murray
Senior Producer Jonathan Wakeham
Managing Editor Sadie Smith
Managing Art Editor Vicky Short
Publisher Julie Ferris
Art Director Lisa Lanzarini
Publishing Director Simon Beecroft

DK would like to thank: Sammy Holland, Michael Siglain, Troy Alders,
Leland Chee, Pablo Hidalgo and Nicole LaCoursiere at Lucasfilm;
Chelsea Alon at Disney Publishing; and Lori Hand
and Jennette ElNaggar for editorial assistance.

First published in Great Britain in 2019 by
Dorling Kindersley Limited
80 Strand, London, WC2R 0RL
A Penguin Random House Company

10 9 8 7 6 5 4 3 2 1
001-315152-May/2019

Page design copyright © 2019 Dorling Kindersley Limited

© & TM 2019 LUCASFILM LTD.

All rights reserved. Without limiting the rights under the copyright reserved above, no part
of this publication may be reproduced, stored in or introduced into a retrieval system,
or transmitted, in any form, or by any means (electronic, mechanical, photocopying,
recording, or otherwise), without the prior written permission of the copyright owner.

A CIP catalogue record for this book is available from the British Library.

ISBN: 978-0-24139-209-6

Printed and bound in China

A WORLD OF IDEAS:
SEE ALL THERE IS TO KNOW
www.dk.com
www.starwars.com